Geronimo Stilton

O9-AHW-164

THE JOURNEY THROUGH TIME

MEDIEVAL MISSION

Scholastic Inc.

ISBN 978-0-545-61129-9

Text by Geronimo Stilton

Original title *Viaggio nel tempo*
Cover by Silvia Bigolin (pencils and inks) and Christian Aliprandi (color)
Illustrations concept by Lorenzo Chiavini, Blasco Pisapia, Roberto Ronchi, and Valeria Turati
Illustrations production by Silvia Bigolin, Danilo Barozzi, Valeria Brambilla, Giuseppe Guindani (pencils and inks), Christian Aliprandi (color), and Francesco Barbieri (appendix)
Graphics by Merenguita Gingermouse, Zeppola Zap, and Yuko Egusa with Chiara Cebraro and Studio Editoriale Littera

Special thanks to AnnMarie Anderson
Translated by Lidia Morson Tramontozzi
Interior design by Kay Petronio

12 11 10 9 8 7 6 5 4 3 2 1   14 15 16 17 18 19/0

Printed in the U.S.A.   40

This edition first printing, September 2014

TRAVELERS ON
THE JOURNEY THROUGH TIME

Dear rodent friends,
My name is Stilton, *Geronimo Stilton*. I am the editor and publisher of *The Rodent's Gazette*, the most famous newspaper on Mouse Island. I'm about to tell you the story of one of my most amazing adventures. Let me introduce you to the other mice you will meet. . . .

THEA STILTON
My sister, Thea, is a special correspondent for *The Rodent's Gazette.* She is very athletic and one of the most stubborn and determined mice I have ever met!

BENJAMIN
My nephew Benjamin is the sweetest and most affectionate little mouselet in the whole world.

TRAP
My cousin Trap is an incredible prankster. His favorite pastime is playing jokes on me.

PROFESSOR PAWS VON VOLT
Professor von Volt is a genius inventor who has dedicated his life to making amazing new discoveries. This time, he built a time machine!

New Mouse City, Present Day

Dear mouse friends,

You are about to read the true tale of the Stilton family's incredible adventure in medieval England! I know it seems impossible, but it isn't. You see, my good friend Professor Paws von Volt invented a **time machine**!

   First, we had an amazing journey to prehistoric times, where I met a baby ~~triceratops~~! Next, Thea, Trap, Benjamin, the professor, and I headed to ancient Egypt, where we discovered how the amazing Great Pyramid at Giza was built.

   Now we're off to ancient

The Mouse Mover 3000

Britain during the reign of King Arthur! We had all climbed into the **Mouse Mover 3000**.

All of us disguised as Egyptians

Professor von Volt set the Chronometer and pressed the departure button. The little ship began to vibrate and filled with a blue mist. . .

"HANG ON TIGHT," the professor shouted. "Here we gooooooo!"

The Chronometer

A CASTLE ON THE HORIZON

When we finally stopped moving, Professor von Volt opened the porthole cautiously.

"Look!" the professor exclaimed. "There's **CAMELOT CASTLE**!"

We climbed out of the Mouse Mover 3000 and gaped at the **ENORMOUSE** castle before us. Once again, the professor reached into his pocket and pulled out five teeny-tiny miniaturized costumes.

Professor von Volt used his secret potion to restore the clothes to their NORMAL size. I pulled on my brown tunic, green coat, striped tights, pointed shoes, leather satchel, and hat with a red feather. Then the professor handed us each five coins.

"I'll give each of you three copper coins, one SILVER coin, and one GOLD coin," he said. "The copper coin can buy you DINNER, the silver coin can buy you a SWORD, and the

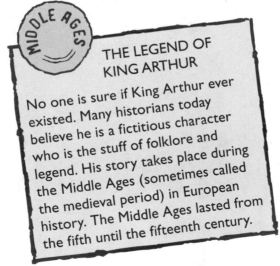

MIDDLE AGES

THE LEGEND OF KING ARTHUR

No one is sure if King Arthur ever existed. Many historians today believe he is a fictitious character who is the stuff of folklore and legend. His story takes place during the Middle Ages (sometimes called the medieval period) in European history. The Middle Ages lasted from the fifth until the fifteenth century.

gold coin can buy you a **HORSE**. Use them well!"

I put the coins in the leather satchel and slipped it across my chest.

We hid the **MOUSE MOVER 3000** behind a rock, covered it with moss, and headed toward the castle.

"We're now in **CAMELOT**, Britain, where, according to legend, the story of King Arthur and the Knights of the Round Table unfolded," Professor von Volt told us. "Our *ADVENTURE* is about to begin!"

MAP OF GREAT BRITAIN

BRITANNIA

The word *Britannia* is Latin and is the ancient name for Great Britain. In the fifth century, Britannia was invaded by Saxon warriors from the northwestern part of modern-day Germany. According to legend, King Arthur led the British defense against the Saxons.

FIFTH CENTURY OR THE TWELFTH CENTURY?

Although King Arthur is believed to have ruled during the fifth century, the most well-known tales of his exploits were written during the twelfth century. These poets and writers used twelfth-century descriptions of scenery and costumes in their work, which is what you'll see depicted here.

Caerleon

BRITANNIA

Tintagel

Avalon

Stonehenge

Camelot

BRITTANY

Brocéliande
(Paimpont forest)

AVALON: The magical island where King Arthur's sword Excalibur was forged and where some believe King Arthur was buried.

CAMELOT: The castle where King Arthur and his court lived.

CAERLEON: City on the Usk River in modern-day Wales that is associated with King Arthur's legendary Round Table.

TINTAGEL CASTLE: King Arthur's birthplace.

BROCÉLIANDE: A legendary forest in the rough location of modern-day Paimpont forest, in Brittany, France, where Merlin's tomb is said to be found.

STONEHENGE: A prehistoric monument of enormous stones built sometime between 3000 and 2000 BC.

Excerpt from the poem
"Idylls of the King"
by Alfred, Lord Tennyson

. . . Then rose the King and
moved his host by night,
And ever pushed Sir Modred,
league by league,
Back to the sunset bound
of Lyonnesse —
A land of old upheaven
from the abyss
By fire, to sink into the abyss again;
Where fragments of forgotten
peoples dwelt,
And the long mountains
ended in a coast
Of ever-shifting sand, and far away
The phantom circle of
a moaning sea . . .

**Feudal lord
or king**

Vassal

Lords

Villeins

Serfs

FEUDALISM

Feudalism was a type of government during medieval times. The **feudal lord** or **king** gave a large estate (called a **fief**) to a **vassal**. In exchange for the land, the vassal agreed to be loyal to the king. The **vassal** would then divide up the land further and give it to his **lords**, who agreed to provide knights who would fight for the king. The lord gave land to the **villeins**, who had to farm the land for the lord. At the very bottom were the **serfs**. They had no land and were considered to be the property of the lord.

CAMELOT? THIS ISN'T CAMELOT!

By the time we reached the castle, the sun had set. The castle was surrounded by a very **deep** moat, and the drawbridge was raised. The flag flying in front of the castle had an image of a *flea* on it. *How odd!*

"Let's pretend to be a troupe of **ACTORS**," Professor von Volt suggested. "That way we'll blend in."

Then he shouted toward the castle: "Hello, citizens of **Camelot**!"

A **tiny** window opened, and a snout appeared.

"Who is it? Who goes there?" the sentry asked. "What does Camelot have to do with anything? This is FLEA FLICKER CASTLE!"

"Whaaaaat?" the professor whispered to us.

"We came to the wrong place. *How odd!*"

"Open the gate! We're actors!" Trap shouted back.

"How do I know you're telling the **truth**?" the sentry asked suspiciously.

Trap began juggling several **COLORED** balls in the air. **POP! POP! POP!** He managed to catch each one and send it into the air again.

POP! POP! POP! POP! POP! POP! POP! POP! POP!

"See?" Trap said. "And my oldest friend here plays the **flute**, the maiden **sings**, and the little one is a **jester**."

The sentry pointed to me.

"What about the one with the **butterflies** on his nose?" he asked.

Butterflies? He must

MIDDLE AGES

EYEGLASSES

Eyeglasses were invented in the thirteenth century in Italy. The monk Alessandro della Spina was the first person to produce them for others. There were many other things that hadn't been invented yet during the Middle Ages, like postage stamps and modern toilets. People used chamber pots instead!

have been talking about my **glasses**.

"I — ahem," I said, taking a step forward, "I'm a minstrel!"

"Really?" the sentry asked. "Then recite a poem!"

Holey cheese! My mind went ⓑⓛⓐⓝⓚ. I couldn't come up with anything!

"Think of something, quick!" Trap whispered as he pinched my tail.

So I improvised:

In the evenings, traveling minstrels entertained citizens with songs that told of courageous heroes, wars, and love.

"Oh, mouse in the castle
Please let us come in,
Our show is so cheesy
You'll laugh and you'll grin!
Our music and jokes
Are better than the rest,
And my rhymes, you can see,
Are simply the best!"

The sentry shook his head.

"Bah, there's nothing **ʃpeciɑl** about that poem, but I'll let you come in anyway," he said. "We're bored. There's nothing to do here. Even if your show **stinks**, it will still be entertaining!"

With a creak, the drawbridge came down. A short, one-eyed mouse with ruffled whiskers came to meet us.

"Follow me," he said. "I'm **Cyclops McMouse.**"

As we followed him through the courtyard, I looked around me. In one corner, a **BLaCKSMiTH** was forging a horseshoe on an anvil. Nearby, a **FarMer** loaded hay on a cart. The **baker** was taking crispy loaves of rye bread out of an oven while an **apprentice** was weaving on a loom inside the tailor's shop.

Cyclops McMouse took us through a maze of **passageways** until we came to a vast hall paved with **BLACK** and **WHITE** stones. Small torches on the walls cast an **EERIE** glow.

CASTLES

Castles had no running water or sewers. The windows were very small and didn't have glass. Curtained canopies hung around the beds and were closed at night to keep in the heat.

There was a glowing *fireplace* at the other end of the hall, but the space was so enormouse that our side of the room was freezing **cold**. Here and there hung embroidered **tapestries** depicting great medieval scenes.

Cyclops McMouse lowered his voice.

"Be careful what you say," he warned. "Sir Flea Flicker isn't a very trusting **mouse**. If he doesn't like the looks of you, he'll chop off your head!"

I was *worried*.

INSIDE THE CASTLE

1. Castle's banner
2. Tower
3. Battlements
4. Arrow slit
5. Drawbridge
6. Moat filled with water
7. Knight
8. Dungeon where prisoners are kept
9. Mechanism to lift the drawbridge
10. Treasury
11. Armor
12. Banquet hall
13. Bedroom
14. Roof
15. Armory
16. Coronation room
17. Sentry
18. Archer
19. Thick brick walls
20. Secret passage
21. Kitchen
22. Pantry

"His son, Flea Flicker Junior, is the same way," Cyclops continued. "He loves to see heads **roll**."

"Oh, I'm not worried," Trap said confidently. "Leave it to me. I'll entertain them with my most **INCREDIBLE** jokes, like this one: What do you call a mosquito in a tin suit? A bite in shining armor! Ha, ha, ha, ha!"

At the end of the hall, I saw a very **LOOONG** table covered with food. Knights were sitting and talking and eating. Some were playing **CHESS**. In a corner, the ladies were busy embroidering as they talked and talked. Sir Flea Flicker, the lord of the castle, was short and stocky with a stubby nose and disheveled fur. He wore a **LOOONG** purple velvet cloak embroidered with little golden fleas that was **stained** with greasy spots.

At his right was his son, Flea Flicker Junior, a big mouse with **greasy** fur, mangy whiskers, and **crooked yellow** teeth.

Cyclops bowed until his whiskers touched the ground.

"Oh, noble sir," he announced loudly. "A troupe of actors has come with the hopes of enlivening this **somber** night!"

I peeked at Sir Flea Flicker to see what effect this introduction might have had. He scratched himself. **Scratch, scratch, scratch!** Then he squashed a flea. **Squish!**

"Humpf!" Sir Flea Flicker mumbled. "If they don't entertain me, **CHOP OFF THEIR HEADS**!"

"Right!" Cyclops McMouse agreed. "If they don't entertain us, **chop, chop**!"

All the knights shouted at the same time: **"Chop, chop, chop!"**

SAY SOMETHING POETIC!

A rat wearing a **BLACK** hood stepped forward.

"There's someone to **decapitate**, huh?" he asked gruffly. "I want to test my new ax!"

He tore out one of his whiskers, tossed it in the air, and cut it with his ax. **CHOP!**

Even Trap looked worried now.

Chop!

Sir Flea Flicker's henchmouse

"Cousin, say something **poetic**, or they'll chop off our heads!" he whispered as he **PINCHED** my tail.

"Don't rush me!" I squeaked. "I can't think when I'm under **PRESSURE!**"

I didn't know what else to say,

so I tried to flatter the mean, scruffy Sir Flea
Flicker:

"Oh, Sir Flea Flicker,
So noble and wise,
We're so glad to meet you,
And all of your guys.
Your castle is mighty,
Your knights are quite brave,
And the cheese that you serve,
The locals all crave!"

"Humpf!" Sir Flea Flicker replied. "Not bad. I
didn't know my cheese was so POPULAR."

I breathed a sigh of relief. We were **saved**!

But then he looked at Trap, Thea, the professor,
and Benjamin.

"What about these four?" he asked suspiciously.
"What can they do?"

Trap began telling joke after joke after
joke.

Q: *Why did the king go to the dentist?*
A: *To get his teeth crowned.*

A knight goes to a shoemaker.
"I would like a pair of boots," he says.
"What color, sir?"
"Both the same, please!"

The lord of the castle meets a friend who lives in a nearby castle.
"Dear friend, can you lend me one hundred pieces of gold?" he asks.
"Oh, I have only one silver coin in my pocket," the friend replies.
"And at the castle?" the lord asks.
"Everyone's fine at the castle, thank you!"

Q: *What king of medieval England was famous because he spent so many nights at his Round Table writing books?*
A: *King Author!*

A knight meets a friend.

"Hello, Sir Mousey," he says. "You've changed so much! You're much thinner than you used to be, your fur is much longer, and your whiskers are blond instead of black."

"My name isn't Sir Mousey," the other knight replies.

The first knight is shocked. "You even changed your name!"

A knight writes to his loved one.

"Fair maiden, I'd cross a thousand enchanted forests to see you again! I'd face a thousand enemy soldiers! I'd fight a thousand ferocious dragons!"

"Well, then, come see me now!" the maiden writes back.

"Now?" the knight writes back. "But it's raining!"

"Tomorrow is my wife's birthday, and I don't know what to get her," one knight tells another.

"Give her a pretty silk handkerchief," the other knight answers.

"Hmmm," the first knight replies. "But I don't know the size of her nose!"

A Food Fight . . .
with Pie!

Professor von Volt began to play a merry melody, Thea sang, and Benjamin danced a little jig.

Danced a little jig... jig... Danced a Danced a little jig... danced a little jig... Danced a little jig...

A procession of servants entered the hall carrying **pewter** dishes of meat, chestnut fritters, quince jelly, blueberry jam, dried figs, and raisins.

Last in line was a TiNY servant around Benjamin's age. He was struggling to carry an **ENORMOUSE** pie that was decorated with a **tiny** flag bearing the Flea Flicker Castle emblem.

As the tiny servant made his way to the table, he tripped on one of the knights' swords and fell. The pie ended up on Sir Flea Flicker's **face**. The lord's snout turned bright red with embarrassment.

"Get that mouse!" he shouted.

To save the little mouselet, Trap grabbed three

Huhhhh!

apples and began juggling them in the air. He was
trying to distract Sir Flea Flicker!
Trap jumped up on a table. He balanced
a spoon on the tip of his snout and spun
a pewter dish on top of the spoon. Meanwhile,
he continued juggling the apples while his
waved the little flag that had been in the pie.

Everyone in the court was AMAZED.

"Hurrah!" they cheered loudly.

Trap put down all of his props. As his grand
FINALE, he took a piece of pie and threw
it in the nearest knight's face.

I held my breath, waiting to see how Sir
Flea Flicker would react. But after a moment
of shock, he laughed so hard he almost choked.
Then he began throwing pieces of pie at his guests.
It was a food fight . . . with pie! Everyone burst
out laughing.

Hee, hee, hee!

Ha, ha, ha!

Ho, ho, ho!

I sighed with relief. The little servant was safe! While the food fight continued, I approached the **trembling** mouselet. He was as PALE as a slice of mozzarella!

"Everything's fine, little one," I reassured him. "Don't be afraid. What's your name?"

"**Crouton**, sir," he replied *softly*. "I'm an orphan. I don't have a mother or father."

As we were talking, a messenger sounded three blasts on a trumpet and handed Sir Flea Flicker a piece of **parchment**.

Toot-toot-toot! Toot-toot-toot!

The trumpeter sounded again:

Toot-toot-toot! Toot-toot-toooooot!

MIDDLE AGES

AT THE TABLE

People ate porridge and other hot cereals, vegetables, black bread, eggs, and wild meat and game caught in the forest. Knives were used to cut the meat, which was then eaten using one's fingers instead of a fork!

"Stop tooting in my ear!" Sir Flea Flicker shouted. "Oof!"

Then he read the parchment.

"Oh, son, get ready!" he shouted with **EXCITEMENT**. "All of Britannia's knights are on their way here, to Flea Flicker Castle. A grand tournament will be held, and the winner will become the **new king**!"

"Papa, are you saying I'll be the next king?" Flea Flicker Junior shouted. "Huh? Huh? Huh?"

MIDDLE AGES

PARCHMENT

The use of paper was not widespread during the Middle Ages. Parchment was used instead. It was made of sheepskin that was soaked in lime, stretched, and then dried. The few books that were in circulation were copied by hand by monastic scribes.

THE IMPOSSIBLE CHALLENGE

Sir Flea Flicker sniffed the air. **Sniff! Sniff!**

"What's that nice smell?" he asked.

Trap bowed down until his WHiSKeRS touched the floor. Then he removed a Gorgonzola cheese sandwich from his satchel.

"It's **GORGONZOLA CHEESE**, my sire!" he said. "Would you like to taste it?"

Sir Flea Flicker gestured to a mouse standing nearby. The **fat** little rodent took the sandwich, smelled it cautiously, and then took a little bite.

Sir Flea Flicker's personal taster

During the Middle Ages, many lords used powerful poisons to kill their rivals. That's why many lords had their own personal tasters. It was that person's duty to try foods before they were given to the lord to make sure they weren't poisoned.

Little **Crouton** leaned toward me.

"That's Sir Flea Flicker's new personal TASTER!" he whispered. "Three have died in the last month."

"So can I eat it?" Sir Flea Flicker asked eagerly.

It is generally believed that John Montagu, fourth earl of Sandwich, invented the sandwich sometime in the late 1700s. According to legend, he frequently asked to be served slices of meat between two pieces of bread so that he didn't have to interrupt his card games to eat a formal meal.

"It's **delicious**, my lord," he said.

"I know it's good," Sir Flea Flicker replied impatiently. "I can smell it! But how do you FeeL?"

"I feel great, sire!" He licked his whiskers.

He tried to take another bite, but Sir Flea Flicker grabbed the sandwich.

"MEDIEVAL MOZZARELLA!" he shouted. "You're supposed to TASTE it, not **eat** it. There'll be nothing left for me!"

Sir Flea Flicker bit into the sandwich and ate the whole thing in just three bites.

"That's quite an appetite!" exclaimed Trap.

Sir Flea Flicker wiped his mouth on his sleeve and let out a belch. **BURP!**

"Hey, you," Sir Flea Flicker said, pointing at Trap. "I nominate you to be the castle's new **COOK**! Prepare a pot of this GORGONSOMETHING-OR-OTHER. I want to look good when the knights come to dine here next week. Make it delicious, or off with your head. *CHOP!*"

Trap snapped to attention.

"Got it, chief!" Trap replied. "There'll be Gorgonzola cheese for the knights that will be whisker-licking good!"

A round rat with curly fur elbowed his way in.

"But I'm the castle cook!" he protested, wielding a wooden spoon.

"Oh, come on!" my cousin squeaked. "I'm better than you! I know a whole BUNCH of things you don't!"

I dare you!

I double dare you!

"Really?" the cook **challenged him**. "Name a food, and I'll cook it — I give you my word!"

"Okay, fine!" Trap replied, a smug look on his snout. "Make me a glass of **orange juice**."

"Hmmm, orange juice?" the rat replied. "Pardon me, but what is that?"

"Okay, make me **TOMATO SAUCE**," Trap said.

"Hmmm, tomato?" the rat replied. "**MEDIEVAL MOZZARELLA**, what is that?"

"Well, then, I'd love a slice of **pineapple**!" Trap replied triumphantly.

"Pineapple? Never heard of it!"

"I bet you that you don't even know how to bake

After the year 1492, a lot of new foods were introduced to Europeans from America. New animals that had been almost entirely unknown to Europeans, such as the modern-day parrot, were also imported from the New World.

a **chocolate** cake, do you?" Trap taunted. "Or make a cup of **COFFEE**?" "**Chocolate**? **COFFEE**?" the cook sobbed. "Never heard of them. That's it! You **won**. You're the better cook!"

Benjamin **CHUCKLED**.

"I told Uncle Trap that tomatoes, pineapples, and chocolate were imported to Europe from **America** after 1492," he told me. "Coffee came from the **Middle East** and the orange came from **CHINA**. That's why no one here in the Middle Ages knows what these foods are yet!"

BRING ME THE GORGONZOLA!

Sir Flea Flicker granted Trap everything he needed to make the Gorgonzola cheese dinner, and he gave Trap permission to go **anywhere** in the castle he wanted.

"Yay!" Benjamin cheered. "This will give us a chance to **explore** the entire castle!"

We chatted with guards, artisans, and farmers, but no one had ever heard of Camelot or KiNG ArtHur.

"It's very odd that the CHRONOMETER didn't take us to Camelot!" Professor von Volt said.

Trap was busy mass-producing Gorgonzola cheese. He used milk in **HUGE** oak barrels that had been rolled into the castle's courtyard from nearby farms. It would be a few days until

the cheese was **ready**.

We knew the cheese was ready by the stinky smell. Sir Flea Flicker descended on the kitchen, **GREEDILY** sniffing the air.

"BRING ME THE GORGONZOLA!"

Trap spread Gorgonzola on some toast. He garnished it with an olive that looked like a flea.

"Ta-da!" Trap exclaimed. "FLEA FLICKER CASTLE'S STINKY TOASTED BREAD!"

The taster barely had time to take a **nibble** and give the okay before Sir Flea Flicker gobbled it up. After he was done, Sir Flea Flicker **dove** into the caldron to eat some more.

"Yummy, yum, yum!" he cried as he came up for air. He was covered in cheese from the tips of his **whiskers** to the end of his **tail**. "Soon all of Britannia's knights will taste and envy my Gorgonzola!"

MERLIN'S EYES

I was sleeping on a straw mat in a corner of the kitchen the next morning near Trap, Thea, Benjamin, and the professor when I woke with a start. The first **rays of the sun** filtered in through a small window, and an imposing figure stood before me. He wore a blue cloak and a tall conical hat with **gold** stars embroidered on it. An owl flew in the window and came to rest on his shoulder with a gentle **rustle**. He smoothed his long white beard and looked at us with **PENETRATING** blue eyes.

"I am Merlin," he GREETED us. "What

MERLIN

According to legend, Merlin was King Arthur's advisor. He was in love with the beautiful young Niviane. He revealed to her all his magical secrets, but she took advantage of that knowledge and locked him in a magical prison, where he perished.

are your names? Are you travelers? I have heard that you have **incredible** magical abilities."

Professor von Volt **BOWED** respectfully.

"So good to meet you, wise Merlin," he replied. "Yes, we are travelers. We come from **FAR, FAR** away."

"I feel that is so," Merlin replied with a nod. "You come from a country outside of reality — unreachable even to me...."

A **SHADOW** passed over his eyes.

"Well, travelers who come from a faraway place, I will tell you a secret," he continued. "In this castle, there is a treasure more precious than **silver** or **gold**. That is why I am here — to reveal the **hidden** treasure so that Britannia can reach its full potential!"

At that moment, a ray of **sunlight** shined directly into my eyes, temporarily blinding me. I rubbed my eyes. When I opened them again, the wizard had **DISAPPEARED**!

Had I been **DreaMiNG**?

"Geronimo, there's a treasure here!" Trap exclaimed. "Let's go find it!"

I guess I was **awake** after all!

"What do you say, Geronimo?" Trap continued. "Even a teeny-tiny treasure would be enough to make this trip worthwhile. Let's **GO**!"

Suddenly, we heard the sound of the trumpet. Toot-toot-toot-tooooooooot!

"Make way for the **bravest** knights in Britanniaaaaaaaa! Make waaaaaaay!"

We glanced out the window.

MIDDLE AGES

CLOTHES

Farmers and other average citizens wore cloth shirts, trousers, leggings, and cloaks. The lords wore embroidered wool or silk clothing dyed bright colors. They were embroidered and decorated with gold, silver, pearls, and precious stones. The lords' clothes were so valuable that they were left to their children as part of their inheritance.

Sure enough, a thick cloud of **dust** covered the road leading to Flea Flicker Castle. Hundreds — no, THOUSANDS — of knights were galloping toward the castle. Each knight carried a **multicolored** banner that waved briskly in the wind. It was an **extraordinary** sight!

Thea quickly snapped a photo. I took out my travel journal and jotted down a few thoughts:

The knights who are to challenge one another for the crown of the King of Britannia are arriving!

"Hurry up, Geronimo," Trap said. "Stop **daydreaming** and help me wash the dishes!"

A MOUSELET WITH GOLDEN BRAIDS

Once I finished washing the dishes, I went to the courtyard to throw out the gàrbàgè.

On my way back into the kitchen, I saw a tiny mouselet with **LONG** blonde braids and a light blue tunic. She wore a silver pendant in the shape of a **heart** with the letter **G** engraved on it.

"That's KING LEODEGRANCE of Carmelide's daughter," I heard someone whisper.

I watched as the little princess strolled toward the stream next to the castle. She went up the **STONE** bridge that crossed the stream. Then she leaned over to watch the *rushing* water below. The knot that held the pendant **loosened**.

The little mouselet tried to grab the necklace, but it fell down into the stream.

Crouton was nearby. Without a hint of hesitation, he jumped into the **frigid** water. A few seconds later, he emerged, holding the pendant. With a bow, he held it out to the mouselet.

"Thank you!" she said, tears of **JOY** in her eyes. "This piece of jewelry is the only remembrance I have of my mother!"

"I understand," Crouton whispered shyly. "I don't have a father or mother."

The two smiled, and I immediately knew they had become friends.

I ran to Crouton and wrapped him in my coat. Even so, his teeth continued to CHATTER.

"Come into the kitchen and warm up by the FIRE, little one," I urged him. He waved good-bye to the golden-haired mouselet, and we went back inside the castle.

FOR MY COUSIN, THAT'S NOTHING!

The next morning I woke to hear the sound of someone sobbing in the courtyard outside the kitchen window. I woke my cousin Trap and **dragged** him outside with me.

"Why'd you have to wake me, Geronimo? **Huh? Huh?**" Trap whined. "I was in the middle of the most **incredible** dream! I had just located the treasure hidden in the castle, and I was **RICH, RICH, RICH**!"

"Shhh!" I shushed my cousin, pointing to a sobbing old rodent leaning against a tree. "That mouse is very **UPSET**. Let's see if we can help.

"Excuse me, sir," I said. "Is everything okay?"

"Oh, my poor, darling Mousilda!" the old rodent sobbed. "I'd save her myself, but alas, I am too **old**! *Brrrrrrrgh!*"

He blew his nose on his coat sleeve.

"I don't understand . . ." I began. Someone tugged **gently** on my tail. It was Crouton!

"Psst, Geronimo," he whispered. "That's Sir Ratford of Cheddarshire. His daughter, Mousilda, is being held **PRISONER** in the tallest tower of the super-scary **BLACK CASTLE**!"

How terrible! I had to do something to help.

"Sir Ratford, my name is Stilton, *Geronimo Stilton*," I told the sad rodent. "I will save your daughter!"

"You will?" he exclaimed, overcome with **joy**. "Thank you, most noble rodent. Thank you!"

He hugged me **TIGHTLY**. My snout turned **PURPLE** with embarrassment.

Um . . .

Noble rodent!

Crouton tugged my tail again.

"Sir Geronimo," he whispered, "are you sure you want to do this? No other knight has dared to enter the **BLACK CASTLE**."

"Of course he dares to save Mousilda!" Trap exclaimed. "My cousin is a very **brave** mouse."

I was? **No, no, no!** I'm not a brave mouse at all! In fact, I'm very, very scared. Back home in New Mouse City, I'm known for being the biggest scaredy-mouse. But if someone needed my help, I couldn't say no.

"But there are strange legends about the **BLACK CASTLE**," Crouton continued. "They say there are gigantic leeches in the moat. . . ."

"Pff, for my cousin, that's nothing!" Trap replied.

"They say there's a **fire-breathing dragon** in the courtyard. . . ."

"Pff, for my cousin, that's nothing!" Trap replied.

The Black Castle

"They say that the Black Knight dumps **boiling hot fondue** on whoever tries to get in. . . ."

"Pff, for my cousin, that's nothing!" Trap replied.

Gigantic leeches

Gigantic leeches? A fire-breathing dragon?? Boiling hot fondue???

Why, why, oh, why had I agreed to come on this wacky journey through time?

A moment later, an enormouse rat in black armor with a face that would scare even a **RABID** cat came galloping up to Flea Flicker Castle on his horse. His coat of arms was a **prancing** black rat with a **forked** tail.

Fire-breathing dragon

Boiling hot fondue

"I am Winston Wickedpaw, from the noble house of Drake Mudrat, also known as the **Black Knight**. I hear that someone here has challenged the great Drake Mudrat!"

Boy, word sure did travel *quickly* in the Middle Ages!

"That's right!" Trap replied boldly. "My cousin *Geronimo Stilton* is going to save the maiden Mousilda."

"Oh, really?" Winston Wickedpaw asked. He turned to me and pointed his super-pointy lance at my snout. "I dare you — no, I **double** dare you to, you measly little mouse!"

"He accepts your challenge!" Trap replied **BOLDLY**. "Make ready your whiskers, Winston Wickedpaw. My cousin Geronimo Stilton will follow you to the **BLACK CASTLE**, where he will defeat **Drake Mudrat** and save the maiden Mousilda! Isn't that right, Geronimo?"

Trap pulled my ear.

"Don't you wimp out now, scaredy-mouse!" he whispered.

WINSTON WICKEDPAW shook his fist at me.

"I'll wait for you at the BLACK CASTLE, Geronimo of Stilton!" he said. "Oooooooh, you're in big trouble! Drake Mudrat is one seriously scary mouse!"

I turned as PALE as a slice of mozzarella. A moment later, I fainted!

BOILING HOT FONDUE SHAMPOO

When I came to, I was wearing a suit of **armor**. Sir Ratford of Cheddarshire and his squires had already dressed me!

"Bring him a horse!" Sir Ratford shouted.

"Yes, of course, bring me a horse," I said. "Wait, what? A horse? I don't know how to ride a horse!"

But Sir Ratford and his squires used a pulley to haul me onto the horse. Then I headed at a gallop toward the **BLACK CASTLE**.

Medieval armor began as chain mail, made of small metal rings linked together. This developed into the more protective plate mail, made of metal plates covering the body along with a metal helmet. Shields were made from wooden planks that were covered in leather and painted.

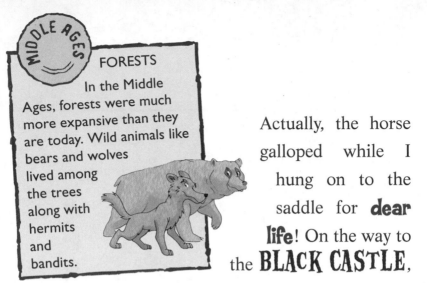

FORESTS

In the Middle Ages, forests were much more expansive than they are today. Wild animals like bears and wolves lived among the trees along with hermits and bandits.

Actually, the horse galloped while I hung on to the saddle for **dear life**! On the way to the **BLACK CASTLE**, I fell off the horse three times! After the third fall, I decided to walk the rest of the way.

It was hard to move through the forest with the armor and sword, so I left them behind. I arrived at the **BLACK CASTLE** at the top of **Black Hill** in the middle of **Black Forest** at night. The creek that ran alongside the castle was **black**. The walls of the castle were **black**, the roof was **black**, the door was **black**, and the banner that flapped on the highest tower was **black**. The cawing crows that gloomily circled the castle's towers were **black**, too.

Caw, caw, caaaaaaaawwwwwww!

Before I got any nearer, I took a deep breath to calm my nerves.

I glanced **worriedly** at the moat, but I didn't see any leeches. So I straightened up, gathered all my COURAGE, and approached the castle.

"Er, is anyone there?" I shouted at the massive **black** door.

A pair of whiskers peered down at me from the top of a tall tower.

"Who goes there?" the guard asked.

"Ahem — I'm the carpenter," I replied. "Someone sent a message about a BROKEN LADDER."

Who goes there?

"In this castle, there's always something rotting away," he grumbled. "Even the roof is falling apart!

"I'm waiting for a **knight**, a certain Geronimo of Stilton," he continued as I followed him inside. "My orders are to drop a caldron of **boiling hot fondue** on his head! Lucky for you, you identified yourself!"

"Lucky me!" I agreed, breathing a secret sigh of **RELIEF**. "I've heard there are some pretty bloodthirsty leeches in the moat. And that fire-breathing dragon must keep things **toasty** warm in the winter!"

The guard chuckled.

Catapult (to hurl stones at the enemy)

"I shouldn't be telling you this because it's a secret, but that rumor about the leeches is just made up to keep **gawkers** away," he said. "And it works, too! No one dares to get anywhere near the castle! Besides, if anyone does come near, I take care of them with a shampoo of **boiling hot fondue**!"

I laughed through gritted teeth.

"Ha, ha, ha," I said. **"Funny!"**

As soon as I could, I slipped away through a **DARK** hallway and went up the stairs that took me to the highest tower.

Ram (used to break down the walls and doors)

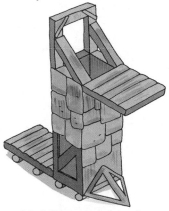

Mobile tower (used to climb up the wall)

OH, I'M SO AFRAID OF HEIGHTS!

I climbed and climbed and climbed. Ugh! Those stairs seemed to go on **FOREVER**!

I got to the tippy top of the tower and saw a ⊤ᴇᴇɴꜱʏ-ᴡᴇᴇɴꜱʏ little **black** door with the Black Knight's coat of arms above it. A thick, rusted key was stuck in the door. I turned it and the little door **SCREECHED** open.

"Do not be afraid, maiden Mousilda!" I cried. "I am here to **save** you!"

I looked around the **black** room. There was a canopied bed with brocaded **black** curtains. Next to the **black** stone fireplace, a melancholy little mouselet with fur as white as snow was busy knitting.

She was dressed in a **GOLD** silk gown and wore a crown studded with rubies. She jumped up.

"Who are you, brave knight?" she squeaked.

I bowed.

"My name is Stilton, *Geronimo Stilton*," I replied. "I'm here to save you!"

I heard the **thud** of heavy footsteps coming up the stairs, and I saw the light of a torch project a dark shadow on the floor. It was **Drake Mudrat**!

We quickly hid behind some armor.

"Mousilda, **WHERE** are you hiding?" Drake Mudrat asked in a **SINGSONG** voice. "Don't you want to marry me, *little mouse of my heart*?"

He peeked behind the brocaded **black** curtains. While he was

Maiden Mousilda

distracted, Mousilda and I SLIPPED out the door and began descending the stairs on tiptoe.

Suddenly, I caught a whiff of stinky garlic.

Achoo! I sneezed loudly.

Drake Mudrat turned. His garlicky breath was making me sneeze uncontrollably!

Achoo, achoo, achoo!

Why, why, oh, why did I have to be allergic to garlic?

"So you've come!" Drake Mudrat shouted as he chased us down the stairs. "I'll catch you, Geronimo of Stilton, and I'll pluck out all your whiskers!"

I heard a clatter from below: SOLDIERS!

Swish!
Swiiiiiiiiish!
Swiiiiiiiiiiiiiiish!

Our only hope was to ESCAPE through a tiny window and get to the roof of the castle. Once we were on the roof, I made the mistake of looking down.

Medieval mozzarella! I'm so afraid of heights!

We were up really, really **HIGH**!

I grabbed Mousilda's paw and, carefully trying to keep our balance, we made our way onto the battlements. Beneath us the archers aimed their **arrows** at us. They flew past us. One **GRAZED** my ear, another **PIERCED** the feather of my hat, while a third arrow **sliced off** one of my whiskers!

Mousilda was wearing a **long** dress that hampered our progress, so I carried her in my arms and ran as fast as I could while I tried **not** to look down.

Grack!

I'm afraid of heights, I'm afraid of heights, I'm afraid of heights, I'm afraid of heights, I'm afraid

I had almost reached the stairs leading to the courtyard when I slipped on a pile of CROW DROPPINGS!

Caw!

Mousilda and I rolled down the roof. Luckily, I grabbed the embankment as we went over the edge. A second later, we were **dangling** high above the ground.

"HEEEEEEEEEEEELP!" we screamed. "Please help us!"

Right below us in the courtyard, I saw four familiar faces. It was Professor von Volt, Thea, Trap, and Benjamin.

"Hang on, Uncle!" Benjamin shouted.

The four of them scampered up the stairs, and seconds later they had grabbed us and pulled us to SAFETY.

MOZZARELLA
PERFUME

"Phew! This time I was sure I was a goner." I sighed. "I thought I would lose my fur!"

We ran **DOWN** the stairs, **CROSSED** the courtyard, and hurried over the drawbridge just as it was beginning to rise. Then we hopped on our horses and **GALLOPED** back toward Flea Flicker Castle.

Mousilda didn't fall off her horse once. Can you guess how many times I fell? **THIRTEEN!** I bruised both **ears**, my right **knee**, my left big **toe**, three **whiskers**, the tip of my **nose**, my left **pinky**, my **tail**, my right **wrist**, my left **incisor** . . . and my **bottom**!

When we finally got back to Flea Flicker Castle, I slid to the floor, **EXHAUSTED**.

Sir Ratford hugged me, tears in his eyes.

"Ask me for anything, anything, absolutely anything you want!" he told me. "Do you want **land**, or a **CASTLE**, or **riches**?"

"Oh, ask for a chest full of **gold**!" Trap whispered excitedly. "Or a coffer full of **PEARLS**!"

"There is no need to give me anything!" I told Sir Ratford.

Sir Ratford took his sword and solemnly laid it first on my **left** shoulder, and then on my **right**.

"Geronimo of Stilton, I name you KNIGHT!" he said. "Do you promise to defend the WEAK and mend the **injustices** in the world?"

"I promise!" I agreed proudly.

"**HOORAY!**" everyone cheered. "Hip, hip, hooray! Three cheers for Geronimo of Stilton!"

"Well done, Uncle!" Benjamin said sweetly.

I heard a *CLICK* and knew my sister was busy snapping photos.

MIDDLE AGES

KNIGHTS

Knights had to respect and obey the Code of Chivalry. The code was a set of rules of honor, and included promises to fight for the welfare of all, protect the weak, to live by honor and for glory, and to always keep one's word.

"Where are you from, my **BRAVE** knight?" Mousilda asked.

"I am from far, far away," I told her. "I will be leaving soon."

"Will you return to Flea Flicker Castle?" she asked.

"**WHO KNOWS?**" I replied. "I may be back some day!"

"Well, then, Sir Geronimo, however far you travel, know that I will always keep the memory of your generous gesture in my **HEART**," she said. "And here's something to help you remember me."

She handed me a white handkerchief that had the *delicate* scent of mozzarella perfume.

I accepted the handkerchief.

"Thank you," I replied humbly. "It would be impossible to forget you, my lady!"

THE GOLD ARROW

The following morning we heard the sound of a trumpet: It was the beginning of the tournament to crown the king of Britannia!

Toot-toot-toot! Toot-toot-toot! Toot-toot-toot! Toooooooooooooooot!

"The tournament will begin with the **archery** competition," the herald announced. "The most valiant shooters will compete for the prize of the **GOLD ARROW**!"

The contestants shot one arrow after another.

When it was **Flea Flicker Junior's** turn, he took aim.

"Now I'll show you how it's done!" he shouted.

He shot three arrows one after another, all

within the target, and closer to the center than anyone else's arrows.

The crowd cheered:

"FLEA FLICKER JUNIOR! FLEA FLICKER JUNIOR! FLEA FLICKER JUNIOR!"

He preened himself.

"Yes, I'm good, and I know it!" he said.

The herald made an announcement: "The winner of the contest is —"

But a voice interrupted him.

"I want to try, too!" came the mouse's squeak.

The contestant came forward, her face covered by the brim of her hat. But I recognized her immediately. It was my sister, **Thea**!

She pushed her hat down so no one would recognize her. Then she notched the arrow and prepared to shoot. **My whiskers trembled with excitement!**

Thea squinted, took aim, and released the arrow. It whistled through the air.

Tournaments took place either on foot or on horses, and knights competed alone or in teams. These spectacular events were originally intended as training for war. Eventually, they became performances for members of the court.

SWISHHHHHHHHHHHHHHHH!

It hit the BULL'S-EYE!

She released another arrow: BULL'S-EYE!

She shot again: BULL'S-EYE!

Thea took off her hat, and everyone recognized her.

bull's-eye

Flea Flicker Junior was **purple** with anger.

"I can't believe she beat me!" he shouted.

"Wow, she's **GOOD** . . ." the crowd murmured.

"She rocks! She's way better than Flea Flicker Junior!"

Thea **accepted** the Gold Arrow as her prize as Trap, Benjamin, Professor von Volt, and I chanted: "*Nothing can stop the Stilton family!*"

MIDDLE AGES

WOMEN

Women did not have the same rights as men during the Middle Ages. Women could not choose their own husbands or inherit land, and they had to obey their fathers and husbands. Still, there were many valiant female figures during the Middle Ages, such as the nun Hildegard of Bingen (1098–1179), a writer, composer, and philosopher; powerful Queen Eleanor of Aquitaine (1122–1204); and the heroic Joan of Arc (1412–1431), who led the French to important war victories.

HEAR YE, HEAR YE, HEAR YE!

At noon, the herald made another announcement:

"Hear ye, hear ye, hear ye! The Grand Rat of Rattonia will **CHALLENGE** Measly Marvin of Mousehampton to a duel."

Two knights came riding into the arena on their steeds. They stopped and waited as their horses pawed **nervously** at the ground. The starting signal sounded, and the knights grabbed their **LONG** lances and galloped toward each other.

The two knights clashed with a **metallic** sound: **Claaaaank!** High in the stands, I saw Crouton **watching** the tournament. I sat down next to him.

"Oh, Sir Geronimo," he gushed. "There are so many knights, and they're so brave!"

TELL ME, WHAT IS YOUR WISH?

Crouton and I spent the entire afternoon watching the tournament. Then **DUSK** fell.

"Tonight is a special night," I explained to Crouton. "It's the night of the *shooting* stars. You can wish upon a star. Tell me, little one, is there something you dream of?"

He **blushed** and shook his head.

"There's nothing?" I asked. "You can tell me."

"I do have one great dream," he whispered. "But it's an **IMPOSSIBLE** dream!"

"Oh, no dream is impossible!" I told him. "Tell me your dream and I promise I'll try to make it come true."

"I . . . ahem . . . I . . ." he whispered. "I want to take part in the **tournament**!"

"Well, as far as I know, the first things you need to have are a **horse** and a **sword**," I said.

Crouton lowered his head **SADLY**.

"I could never afford a horse," he said.

I opened my satchel. I took out the **GOLD COIN** Professor von Volt had given me.

"With this coin, you can get yourself the best horse in **Britannia**!" I said as I handed it to Crouton.

"Really?" Crouton asked in surprise. "Thank you, Sir Geronimo!"

I reached in my satchel again.

"And then, dear Crouton, you can use this **silver coin** to buy a sword."

"Thank you, Sir Geronimo, but I already found a sword," he said. "It's wedged in a rock."

"Stuck in a rock?" I asked, disbelieving.

He clasped my paw and led me to the **TOWN SQUARE**.

PAWS OFF THE SWORD!

"Here's the sword!" Crouton squeaked.

I saw a SHINING blade wedged in a rock. Little Crouton grabbed it with both little paws and lifted it above his head proudly.

"Hey, you!" someone grunted. "Where did you get that sword?"

It was Flea Flicker Junior. He grabbed Crouton's sword.

"It's . . . it's . . . it's Excalibur!" he shouted excitedly. "Hey, everyone. Come look! Get ready to meet and crown the new king of Britannia!"

I took a step forward.

"Ahem . . . Sir Flea Flicker Junior, the sword actually belongs to little Crouton," I said. "He's the mouse who DREW it from the stone."

Flea Flicker Junior **grunted** contemptuously. **"IMPOSSIBLE!"** he scoffed. "I wouldn't believe it even if I saw it! And anyway, I have the sword now, and I'm keeping it. **PAWS OFF!"**

Sir Flea Flicker pushed through the crowd.

"My son!" he exclaimed. "You finally did something right! Great news: The tournament's over. My son has the *Sword from the Stone* and will be king of Britannia!"

Trap, Thea, Benjamin, Professor von Volt, and I stood by Crouton.

"The sword belongs to Crouton!" the professor said firmly.

All the knights crowded around the sword.

"Is it true?" they murmured. "Is it really Excalibur?"

"Someone took it out of the **STONE**!"

"Yes, it was a tiny servant. . . ."

"No, it was Flea Flicker Junior. . . ."

"At least that's what he says. . . ."

"I can't see him as **KING**. . . ."

"But no one saw him pull the **SWORD** out of the stone. . . ."

"I think this is just a prank. . . ."

Suddenly, the great Merlin appeared. He made a sign asking for SILENCE.

"Knights of Britannia, do you want a king?" he asked. "If you do, the **SWORD** will choose him."

The crowd gathered in the square. At the center of the square was a massive dark granite stone.

Merlin read the words carved in the stone:

THE MOUSE WHO EXTRACTS THIS
SWORD SHALL BECOME THE RIGHTFUL
KING OF BRITANNIA

"Give me Excalibur!" Merlin ordered

Flea Flicker Junior.

The mouse handed over the sword reluctantly.

Merlin put it back in the stone.

Flea Flicker Junior stepped up to the sword.

"Moooooove!" he ordered those in his way. "In just a moment, I'll be king!"

He grabbed the hilt of the sword and pulled with all his might. He pulled and pulled and pulled . . . but nothing happened!

"Pull, pull, pull!" his father squeaked. "Come on, son, puuuuuuuull!"

Flea Flicker Junior dried his sweat-soaked whiskers.

"I can't, Daddy," he sobbed. "I really can't!"

"Step aside," Sir Flea Flicker said. "I'll show you how to do it!"

Panting, he pulled and

Grunt!

Grunt!

Grunt!

pulled and pulled . . . but the sword didn't **BUDGE** an inch.

"I want to try!" one of the knights shouted.

One after another, all the knights tried to extract the sword.

Sylvester Strongmouse of Stalwart, the strongest knight in Britannia, tried to extract the sword, but it didn't budge an inch!

Robert Roundmouse of Stoutville, the roundest knight, tried next. But in spite of his

Sylvester Strongmouse of Stalwart

Robert Roundmouse of Stoutville

Wilson Wisemouse of Wisdomshire

Richard Reekrat of Stinkonia

weight, the sword didn't budge an inch!

Wilson Wisemouse of Wisdomshire, the oldest of the knights, also tried. But in spite of his wisdom, the sword didn't budge an inch!

Finally, *Richard Reekrat of Stinkonia* tried as well. Because of his odor, they left him for last. And you guessed it — the sword didn't budge an inch!

When everyone had stepped aside, disappointed, we heard a LiTTLe voice.

"Can I try, too?" Crouton asked.

Sir Flea Flicker and his son laughed.

"Look here," Sir Flea Flicker **SCOFFED**. "It's Crouton the servant."

I took a step forward.

"**Let HiM tRy!**" I said firmly.

"Sure, let him try," Flea Flicker Junior sneered. "I could use a good **laugh**!"

THE SWORD THAT SINGS

I walked with Crouton to the center of the square. He took a few **timid** steps toward the stone where the sword was **WEDGED**. When he got to the stone, he hesitated and turned toward me.

"Go on, little one," I encouraged him. "It's your turn. You can do it!"

He grasped the hilt of the sword, and . . . he pulled the sword out of the stone **EFFORTLESSLY**.

"Ooooooooooooooooooooooh!" the crowd gasped.

A ray of moonlight pierced the clouds. The sword sang **sweetly**:

"I am the Sword in the Stone,
And you are the heir to the throne.
The King of Britannia you'll be,
This is my solemn decree!"

"It's a trick!" Flea Flicker Junior shouted. "He's just a servant, so it doesn't COUNT! It's a trick!"

"Yes, yes!" the crowd shouted. "It must be one of Merlin's tricks!"

"The magician's paw must be in it!"

Crouton placed the SWORD back in the STONE. Then he took it out again and raised it over his head so that everyone could see. This time, there was no doubt. Merlin made a solemn gesture and raised his arms to the SKY.

"Hear ye, hear ye!" Merlin shouted. "Years have passed since our king Uther Pendragon left us forever. But today we are gathered here to CROWN his legitimate heir: his son, Arthur. Long live Britannia's new king! Long live KING ARTHUR!"

The crowd knelt down on the ground.

"Long live the new King of Britannia!"

Excalibur!

they all shouted. "Long live King Arthur!"

The sword blazed and the crowd chanted:

"Ar-thur! Ar-thur! Long live King Arthur!"

The little mouselet with the blonde braids gazed at Crouton — that is, Arthur — with adoring eyes.

Arthur blushed **shyly**.

"My lady!" he greeted her.

She gave him her arm, and the two walked toward the castle, gazing into each other's eyes.

"Ah, Maiden Guinevere and little **ARTHUR** look so cute together. . . ." I heard some gossipers whisper.

Merlin smiled with satisfaction.

"That was the treasure hidden in the castle: a great king. **KING ARTHUR!**"

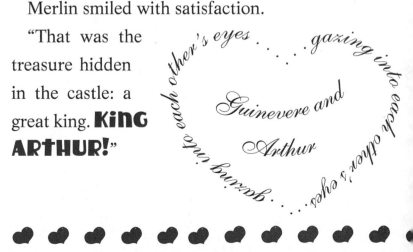

The Knights of the Round Table

According to legend, King Arthur was the secret son of the King of Britain, Uther Pendragon, and Lady Igraine, duchess of Tintagel. His half sister was Morgan le Fay. When King Pendragon died, Merlin the magician hid little Arthur in a faraway castle to protect him. When Arthur was ready to ascend the throne, Merlin revealed that he was the true king through the Sword in the Stone. Guinevere, daughter of King Leodegrance, married Arthur. Under the sage rule of King Arthur, Britain fought off the Saxon invaders. Finally, Merlin gave King Arthur one final mission: to find the Holy Grail. Supposedly, the cup held the cure to many ailments and it bestowed its owner with great wisdom. King Arthur gathered the most valiant knights around his Round Table, which was designed without a head to signify that all who sat at the table shared an equal status. He then asked for their help locating the Holy Grail. According to the legend, no one knows for sure if Arthur or his knights ever found it.

A NEW KING AND QUEEN

Suddenly, Professor von Volt ran up to me, panting and OUT OF BREATH.

"Geronimo, where have you been?" he asked. "I've been looking for you. We have to leave immediately. The **MOUSE MOVER 3000'S** batteries are almost out of power! If we don't leave soon, we may have to stay here **FOREVER**!"

"Will little Crouton be okay?" I asked Merlin, concerned for my young friend.

"Yes, dear *friend*," he replied. "I will make it my responsibility to advise him and to make him a good king.

"I do think the castle will need a new name, though.

The future king and queen

Flea Flicker Castle is a **horrible** name. I'll advise him to call it . . . CAMELOT! I think Camelot will soon have a new queen, Guinevere, that sweet little mouselet."

Professor von Volt smiled.

"Arthur, Guinevere, Camelot . . . **GOOD**!" he said. "Now everything makes sense."

Merlin raised his paw to bid us farewell.

"I won't forget you, travelers from afar!" he said.

We climbed aboard the Mouse Mover 3000.

"Ready?" squeaked Professor von Volt.
"*Goooooooooo!*"

The time machine jolted.

PANGGGGGGGGGGGGGGGGGGGGG!!!

Soon we were back in New Mouse City.

Ah, it felt so good to be home!

I GIVE YOU
MY WORD . . .

We found ourselves back in Professor von Volt's laboratory. The door opened and my friends and I climbed out of the time machine. Ah, HOME SWEET HOME!

I couldn't wait to get home and take a warm, cheddar-scented bath.

"Oh, wait!" Trap yelled. "I left my bag on the ship! Geronimo, can you get it for me? I'm late for an APPOINTMENT!"

"An appointment?" I grumbled as I climbed back inside the Mouse Mover 3000, whose batteries were charging. "When did you have time to make an APPOINTMENT while the rest of us were busy traveling through time? This better not be another one of your tricks, Trap!"

Whoopsie!

"Who, me? Do **tricks**?" Trap asked. "Be real, Geronimo. I'm the most **serious** mouse of all time! You're so **SUSPICIOUS**. It's not good for your **HEALTH**, you know? Anyway, gotta go! See you later, alligator!"

With that, he dashed out the door. As he was running out, he *TRIPPED* on something on the floor. It was the **remote control** for the **MOUSE MOVER 3000**.

Suddenly, the Mouse Mover 3000 began to **HUM**, and the door closed with a bang. This time, I knew what was happening. So I quickly buckled my seat belt and inserted the earplugs. The time machine filled with

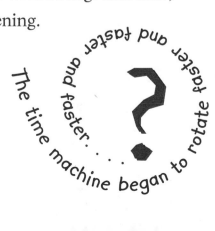

The time machine began to rotate faster and faster and faster. . . . ?

a BLUE fog and began rotating *faster* and *faster*! Where was I going? I didn't know. But I wasn't worried. In fact, I was excited about traveling through time **again**. Who knew what adventure I might find!

Maybe I would end up in ancient Greece, where I would chat with great philosophers like PLATO and ARISTOTLE. Or maybe I would find myself in ancient Rome, where I could take part in a chariot race in the Coliseum. Or perhaps I would travel to the year 1492 to see Christopher Columbus set foot in America!

Ah, philosophy!

Oh, the chariot races . . .

Where would the Mouse Mover 3000 take me? **WHERE? WHERE? WHERE?????????????**

I held on tight and —

BANGGGGGGGGGGGGG!

The time machine came to a sudden **stop**. I had a feeling I was about to have another WHiSKeR-LiCKiNg-gooD adventure!

I give you my word that whatever happens on my journey, I'll be sure to write about it . . . **someday**!

Until then, farewell, *dear mouse friends*!

Maybe I would see Christopher Columbus!

Dear rodent friends,

I hope you have enjoyed reading all about my adventures during my journey through medieval England. To keep the memories fresh, I wrote this very special **travel journal** just for you. It's full of FUN FACTS and **definitions**.

Learn about the secrets of a medieval castle and take a special quiz to find out which era in time you're best suited for. You'll find it's like taking off again on a fabumouse journey through time!

Geronimo Stilton

Middle Ages Fun Facts

- The largest medieval castle in central Europe is the **Spiš Castle** in eastern Slovakia, which is now partially in ruins.

- It usually took around **seven to twelve years** to build a medieval castle. Some larger castles, like the Tower of London, were rebuilt and added on to for hundreds of years.

- **Château Gaillard** is a medieval castle in Normandy, France, that was built by Richard the Lionheart beginning in 1196. Remarkably, the castle was constructed in just two years.

- The oldest standing castle in Europe is part of the **Château de Doué-la-Fontaine** in western France. The castle is believed to have been the first European castle built out of stone, in around 950.

MIDDLE AGES
MINI DICTIONARY

amanuensis: A medieval monk or servant whose job it was to write books from dictation by hand and illustrate them with miniature drawings.

arrow slit: A thin vertical cutout opening in a castle wall that archers can use to launch arrows at invading forces. Also called an *arrow loop* or *loop hole*.

coronation: The ceremony in which a king, queen, or other ruler is crowned.

jester: A professional joker or entertainer in medieval courts.

joust: A competition between two knights on horseback with lances.

lance: A long spear with a pointed metal tip, used in the past by soldiers fighting on horseback.

maiden: A young, unmarried woman.

minstrel: A musician or someone who recited poems in medieval times.

parchment: Heavy sheets of paperlike material made from the skin of sheeps, goats, or other animals and used for writing.

pewter: A metal made of tin mixed with lead or copper. Pewter is used to make plates, pitchers, and other utensils.

sentry: A person who stands guard and warns others of danger.

standard: The flag or banner of a nation or military group.

The Secrets of the Castle

SPIRAL STAIRCASES were steep, narrow, and always turned upward in a clockwise direction from the bottom. This was so that an attacker who was coming up the stairs while holding a sword in his right hand couldn't make the best use of the sword because his arm would hit the castle wall.

A **HOARDING** was a temporary shedlike wooden structure built on top of the exterior walls of a castle during a battle. The hoarding protected soldiers who were firing arrows directly down the wall of the castle toward attackers at the wall base.

The **KEEP** was a remote, fortified tower built within the castle that served as a refuge of last resort if an enemy overtook the rest of the castle.

A **PORTCULLIS** was a latticed grille made of wood or metal that was mounted in vertical grooves in the castle walls. It could be raised or lowered quickly using chains or ropes attached to a winch in order to securely close off the castle during an attack.

The **EXTERIOR WALLS** that surrounded the castle often had walkways along the top to allow defenders to move quickly around the castle.

QUIZ!

In which historical period would you have lived?

1 At the end of dinner, which dessert would you choose?
   a) A pistachio ice-cream cone
   b) An almond and honey pastry
   c) A slice of wild berry pie

2 What do you do if you don't agree with someone else's opinion?
   a) You get angry.
   b) You try to find a compromise.
   c) You make your point of view known through a conversation.

3 What are your favorite subjects?
   a) History and geography
   b) Math and geometry
   c) English and drawing

4 Which color do you like the most?
   a) Green
   b) Yellow
   c) Blue

5 Which of these places would you most like to visit?
   a) A tropical forest
   b) The desert
   c) An abandoned castle

6 What profession interests you the most?
   a) Geologist (someone who studies the earth's physical structure, especially soil and rocks)
   a) Archeologist (someone who studies the past, often by digging up and examining the remains of old buildings, objects, and bones)
   a) Philologist (someone who studies literature, history, and classic languages)

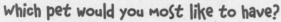

7 Which pet would you most like to have?
   a) A prehistoric fish
   b) A cat
   c) A horse

8 What's your favorite way to spend an afternoon with a friend?
   a) Flying a kite at the park
   b) Playing at home
   c) Drawing or writing stories together

9 Which type of house would you like most?
- **a)** A tree house
- **b)** A palace
- **c)** A small country home

10 Where would you most like to live?
- **a)** At the foot of a mountain
- **b)** Near a river
- **c)** On a small, rolling hill

11 If you were invited to a birthday party, what would you wear?
- **a)** Comfortable everyday clothes
- **b)** Something fun and fancy
- **c)** Anything, as long as it matches

In what period would you have lived?

HERE ARE THE RESULTS...

Prehistoric

If you answered **A** to most questions, you are adventurous and can always get out of a tricky situation. You probably would have most liked living in the prehistoric era.

Egyptian

If you answered **B** to most of the questions, you are detail-oriented, patient, and calm, and you solve problems with a lot of thought and care. You probably would have most liked living in ancient Egypt.

Medieval

If you answered **C** to most of the questions, you have a vivid imagination but you are also a rational thinker. You probably would have most liked living in the Middle Ages, where you would have been a faithful advisor to the king.

Check out all of my journeys through time!

#1: DINOSAUR
DISASTER

#2: PYRAMID
PUZZLE

#3: MEDIEVAL
MISSION

Don't miss any of my other fabumouse adventures!

#1 Lost Treasure of the Emerald Eye

#2 The Curse of the Cheese Pyramid

#3 Cat and Mouse in a Haunted House

#4 I'm Too Fond of My Fur!

#5 Four Mice Deep in the Jungle

#6 Paws Off, Cheddarface!

#7 Red Pizzas for a Blue Count

#8 Attack of the Bandit Cats

#9 A Fabumouse Vacation for Geronimo

#10 All Because of a Cup of Coffee

#11 It's Halloween, You 'Fraidy Mouse!

#12 Merry Christmas, Geronimo!

#13 The Phantom of the Subway

#14 The Temple of the Ruby of Fire

#15 The Mona Mousa Code

#16 A Cheese-Colored Camper

#17 Watch Your Whiskers, Stilton!

#18 Shipwreck on the Pirate Islands

#19 My Name Is Stilton, Geronimo Stilton

#20 Surf's Up, Geronimo!

#21 The Wild, Wild West

#22 The Secret of Cacklefur Castle

A Christmas Tale

#23 Valentine's Day Disaster

#24 Field Trip to Niagara Falls

#25 The Search for Sunken Treasure

#26 The Mummy with No Name

#27 The Christmas Toy Factory

#28 Wedding Crasher

#29 Down and Out Down Under

#30 The Mouse Island Marathon

#31 The Mysterious Cheese Thief

Christmas Catastrophe

#32 Valley of the Giant Skeletons

#33 Geronimo and the Gold Medal Mystery

#34 Geronimo Stilton, Secret Agent

#35 A Very Merry Christmas

#36 Geronimo's Valentine

#37 The Race Across America

#38 A Fabumouse School Adventure

#39 Singing Sensation

#40 The Karate Mouse

#41 Mighty Mount Kilimanjaro

#42 The Peculiar Pumpkin Thief

#43 I'm Not a Supermouse!